A Very Special Wish

A Collection of Stories to Share

Contents

The
Wish
Cat

Ragnhild Scamell

illustrated by Gaby Hansen

Holly's house had a cat flap.
It was a small door in the big
door so a cat could come and go.

But Holly didn't have a cat.

One night, something magical
happened. Holly saw a falling star.
As the star trailed across the sky, she
made a wish.

"I wish I had a kitten," she whispered.
"A tiny cuddly kitten who could jump
in and out of the cat flap."

13

CRASH!

Something big landed on the windowsill outside.
It wasn't a kitten . . . .
It was Tom, the scruffiest, most raggedy
cat Holly had ever seen. He sat there in
the moonlight, smiling a crooked smile.

"Meo-o-ow!"

"I'm Tom, your wish cat," he seemed to say.

"It's a mistake," cried Holly.
"I wished for a kitten."
Tom didn't think Holly had
made a mistake.

16

He rubbed his torn ear against the window and howled so loudly it made him cough and splutter.

"Meo-o-ow, o-o-w, o-o-w!"

Holly hid under her covers, hoping that he'd go away.

The next morning, Tom was still there, waiting for her outside the cat flap. He wanted to come in, and he had brought her a present of a smelly old piece of fish.

"Yuck!" said Holly. She picked it up and dropped it in the garbage can. Tom looked puzzled. "Bad cat," she said, shooing him away.

"Go on, go home!" said Holly, walking over to her swing.

19

But Tom was there before her. He sharpened his claws on the swing . . .

and washed his coat noisily, pulling out bits of fur and spitting them everywhere.

At lunchtime, Tom sat on the
windowsill, watching Holly eat.

She broke off a piece of her sandwich and
passed it out to him through the cat flap.
Tom wolfed it down, purring all the while.

In the afternoon, a cold wind swept through the garden, and Holly had to wear her jacket and scarf. Tom didn't seem to feel the cold. He followed her around . . .

chasing leaves . . .

balancing along the
top of the fence . . .

showing off.

Soon, it was time for
Holly to go inside.
    "Bye, Tom," she said, and
stroked his scruffy head.

Tom followed her to the
door and settled himself
down by the cat flap.

That evening, it snowed.
Sparkly flakes of snow
danced in the air.
Outside the cat flap,
Tom curled himself into a
ragged ball to keep warm.
Soon, there was a white
cushion of snow all over
the doorstep, and on Tom.

Holly heard him meowing miserably.
She ran to the cat flap and held it open.

Tom came in, shaking snow all over
the kitchen floor.

"Poor old Tom," said Holly.

He ate a large plate of food, and drank
an even larger bowl of warm milk.
Tom purred louder than ever when
Holly dried him with the kitchen towel.

Soon, Tom had settled down,
snug on Holly's bed.
Holly stroked his scruffy fur,
and together they watched
the glittering stars.

Then, suddenly, another star
fell. Holly couldn't think of
a single thing to wish for.
She had everything she
wanted. And so did Tom.

The Very Busy Day

Diana Hendry

Jane Chapman

It was a hot, sunny day, and Big Mouse was digging in the garden.

38

SWISH!

Little Mouse sat on the swing, wearing his sun hat.

"There's a lot of digging to do," said Big Mouse. "Come and help me, Little Mouse."

"I'm too busy to help," said Little Mouse. "I'm dreaming up something."

And he swung up and down, up and down.

39

"You could put in these seeds,"
said Big Mouse. "If you plant them
in the dark, they'll dream up flowers."

SWISH!

"Umm," said Little Mouse, "I've got my own dream, and I'm busy thinking about it."

"Busy doing nothing," grumbled Big Mouse.

41

WHEEE!

Little Mouse slid off the swing
and jumped into the wheelbarrow.
He lay and gazed at the sky.
"I need that wheelbarrow
for the weeds," said Big Mouse.
"And look at the mess you've made."

43

MANSION POLISH

3

Big Mouse tipped Little Mouse
out on to the grass. "Please,
Little Mouse, I need some help."

"I'm too busy to help," cried
Little Mouse, and he ran off to
pick some daisies.

Big Mouse picked up all the
weeds. He wiped his forehead
and rubbed his back.
"Phew, it's hot," he puffed.

"And this wheelbarrow's very
heavy all of a sudden."
It was heavy because Little
Mouse had jumped back in!
He was sitting on top of the
weeds, making a daisy chain.

CREAK!

"I'm not pushing you and the weeds," said Big Mouse indignantly. "Out you go! Come and help me take the weeds to the garbage dump." Little Mouse hung the daisy chain around his neck and scrambled out of the wheelbarrow.

But he didn't help
Big Mouse. He picked
lots and lots of clover
instead. He put the
clover in a flowerpot
on the back doorstep.

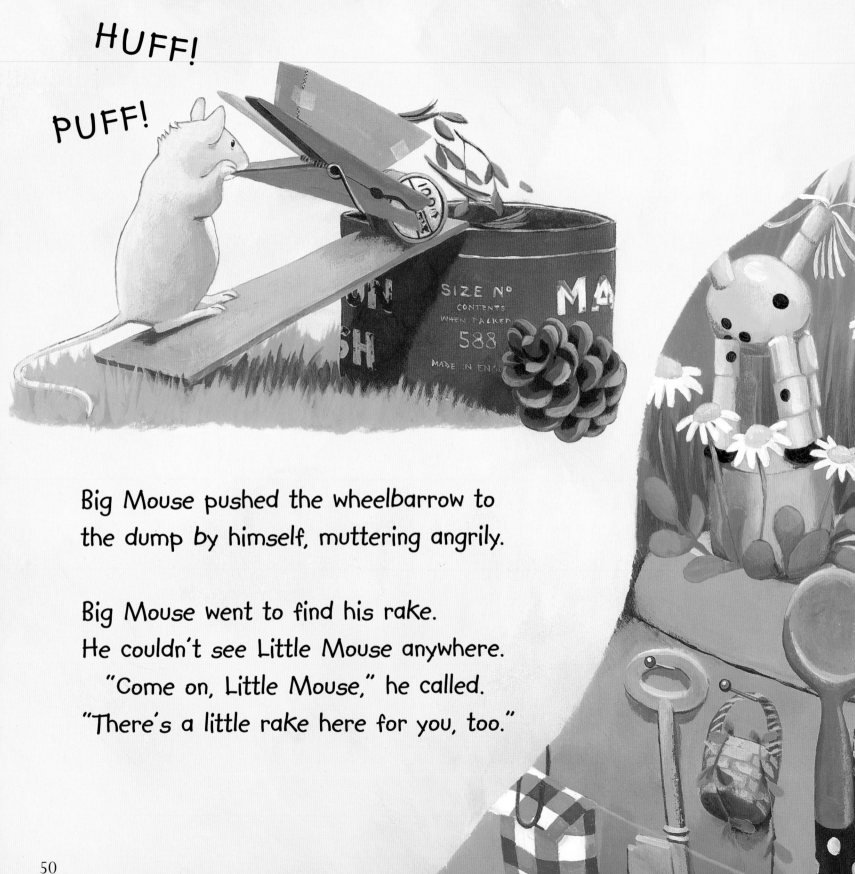

HUFF!

PUFF!

Big Mouse pushed the wheelbarrow to
the dump by himself, muttering angrily.

Big Mouse went to find his rake.
He couldn't see Little Mouse anywhere.
"Come on, Little Mouse," he called.
"There's a little rake here for you, too."

ON POLISH

As Big Mouse climbed down the ladder, Little Mouse poked his head out. "Can't you see I'm busy?" he called. "I'm collecting birds' feathers. This dream is very hard work." "Humph!" said Big Mouse. "There's dreaming and there's doing. What about a little *doing* from you!"

HUMPH!

Little Mouse had found
three snowy white feathers.
He laid them carefully
on the doorstep.

54

By now, Big Mouse
was busy. "Little Mouse,"
he called. "You could help
me carry this strawberry
down the ladder."

"Can't stop now," said
Little Mouse. "I need
something from the
kitchen."

The sun had made Big
Mouse's head ache, and he
felt very angry with Little
Mouse for not helping him.
"What's he doing now?"
he grumbled.

Little Mouse rushed out into the garden. "Big Mouse, Big Mouse," he called. "Look what I've made for you!"

"It's your very own special sun hat!"
"Oh, thank you, Little Mouse!" said
Big Mouse, putting it on his head.
"Now I can see why you've been
so busy dreaming. It's my very
own special Dream Hat!"

"We've both been very busy,"
said Little Mouse, yawning.
"There's just time to do one
more thing," said Big Mouse . . .

". . . and that's to have a nice long snooze!"
Big Mouse and Little Mouse curled up together underneath the leaves. Little Mouse's hat fell off, and Big Mouse's hat slid right down over his nose.

60

The Most Precious Thing

Gill Lewis

Illustrated by Louise Ho

Little Bear was taking Mommy Bear on a walk through the forest in the autumn sunlight. She wanted to show her the special place where the juiciest berries and the sweetest nuts could be found.

As Little Bear skipped through
the rustling leaves, she suddenly
spied a small blue stone glittering
in the sunshine.

"Look, Mommy, look!" cried Little Bear, picking it up. "Look at this shiny jewel I found."
Little Bear gazed as it sparkled in her paw. "It must be the most precious thing in the whole wide world," she gasped.

"Oh yes, Little
Bear, this is a very
beautiful stone," said
Mommy Bear, holding it up
so that it twinkled in the light,
"but the most precious thing is
even prettier than this."

70

"Really?" said Little Bear in wonder. She
put the stone carefully in her bag. "Let's go
and look! I want to find the most precious
thing EVER!"

"Wait for me," laughed Mommy Bear, as
Little Bear scampered off through the trees.

Little Bear and Mommy Bear played games in the afternoon sun. They tried to catch the seeds that spun in the breeze. And Little Bear kept looking for something prettier than the little blue stone.

After a while, they came to Little Bear's special place, and they filled their tummies with juicy purple blackberries. Little Bear was reaching for a berry when she saw something pink hidden in the bushes . . . .

It was a beautiful wild rose.

"Mommy!" shouted Little Bear excitedly. "Come and see what I found!"

She stroked the rose's silky petals and sniffed its sweet smell. "I've never seen such a pretty flower. Surely this must be the most precious thing?"

"This rose is very pretty, Little Bear," said
Mommy Bear, "and it's soft as velvet." She
tickled the rose against Little Bear's nose,
making her sneeze. "But the most precious
thing is even softer than this."

Little Bear wondered what on Earth could be softer than her beautiful rose. She searched and searched through the dry, crunchy leaves, but she found only spiky horse chestnuts, bristly pinecones, and a rather cross hedgehog!

Just then she caught sight of something fluttering high up in the trees.

"Look up there!" she shouted. "That *has* to be it!"

Mommy Bear lifted Little Bear up
into the air. Caught in a spider's
web was a tiny, fluffy feather. Little
Bear reached up high and took the
feather very gently in her paw.

Little Bear touched the downy feather against her cheek.

"Oh, Mommy," she whispered hopefully. "Please tell me. Is this the most precious thing?"

"It is very soft," said Mommy Bear, "but the most precious thing is even better than this — it makes me want to dance for joy."

And Mommy Bear twirled Little Bear around, making her giggle.

Little Bear was determined
to find the most precious thing.
She ran up a grassy hilltop to
look out at the woods and
fields. Hundreds of dazzling
butterflies suddenly filled the
air around her.

One of the butterflies landed
lightly on her paw. Little Bear
gazed at it in wonder.

"This is it!" she sang out
happily. "At last, I have found
the most precious thing in
the whole wide world."

Little Bear and Mommy Bear lay in the long grass as the butterfly fluttered through the golden sunlight.

"Oh yes, that is very special," said Mommy Bear softly, "but I can hold the most precious thing safe and tight in my arms."

"Oh, please tell me what it is!" said Little Bear crossly. "I have looked everywhere and I still haven't found it."

Mommy Bear smiled. "The most precious thing is prettier than any jewel, softer than a rose or the fluffiest feather, and fills me with more joy than a dancing butterfly. The most precious thing . . ." she said, hugging Little Bear tightly, ". . . is you!"

Mouse, Mole,
and the Falling Star

A. H. Benjamin   John Bendall-Brunello

Mole and Mouse were the best of friends. They had fun together.

They shared everything.

They trusted each other completely, even with their deepest secrets.

When one was sad or not feeling well the other was always there to comfort him.

That's how much they loved each other.
"I'm lucky to have a friend like you," Mole would say.

"No," Mouse would reply.
"I'm lucky to have a friend like *you*!"

One summer evening, Mole and Mouse lay side by side on top of a hill, gazing at the starry sky.

"Aren't stars beautiful?" sighed Mole happily.

"Yes," said Mouse. "And magical, too. They sometimes fall from the sky, you know. And if you ever find a fallen star, your wishes will come true."

"Wow!" said Mole. "Then you could wish for anything in the world and you would have it."

"That's right," said Mouse dreamily. "Just imagine that!"

Mole and Mouse fell silent
for a moment, dreaming of
magic stars and all the things
they could wish for.

Just then, a shooting star zipped across the
sky. One moment it was there, and the next,
it was gone.

"Did you see that?" gasped Mole, sitting up.

"Yes, I did," cried Mouse. "It's a fallen star,
and I'm going to find it!"

Mouse scrambled to his feet and
scurried quickly down the hill.
    "Wait!" called Mole, racing after him.
"It's my star! I saw it first."
    "No, I saw it first!" shouted Mouse.
"It's *my* star!"

When they reached the bottom of the hill, Mole and Mouse started searching for the fallen star. Each one hoped he would find it first. But neither did.

"Maybe the star fell in the woods," thought Mouse. "I'll go and look for it tomorrow."

Mole stared toward the woods, too. He was thinking exactly the same thing.

But they did not tell each other,
and they went back to their homes
without even saying good-night.

The next day before sunrise, Mole sneaked out of his house and set off toward the woods.

A few minutes later, Mouse did the same.

104

Mouse and Mole spent the entire morning in the woods,
looking for the fallen star. Once or twice, they spotted
each other. But they pretended they hadn't.

Then, in the afternoon, Mole came across a small patch of charred grass.

"Maybe this is where the star has fallen," he thought. "But someone's already taken it. It can only be Mouse!"

A little later, Mouse came across the same charred
patch of grass. He thought the star had fallen there, too.
   "It's gone!" he cried. "And I bet I know who's taken it.
It has to be Mole!"

As darkness fell, both Mole and Mouse went their separate ways home, each feeling very angry with the other. They did not speak to each other again, except to argue.

"You stole my star!" Mole yelled.

"No, *you* stole *my* star!" Mouse
yelled back.

Mole didn't trust Mouse, and
Mouse didn't trust Mole.

So, Mole sneaked into Mouse's house to find the star . . .

and later on, Mouse looked through Mole's window to see where Mole had hidden it.

But neither found the fallen star.

The days rolled by, and summer was nearly
over. Mole and Mouse grew lonely and miserable.
They missed each other's company, the fun they
used to have together, the secrets they had shared.
They even missed the sad moments.

"Mole can keep the star if he wants," thought Mouse.
"All I want is my friend back."
"If I had never seen that star, Mouse would
still be my friend," thought Mole.

Soon the fallen star became
just a sad memory — until
one day . . . .

Mouse was climbing up the hill when he spotted a golden leaf, swirling and twirling in the air.

"It's the fallen star!" he cried. "Mole must have lost it. I'll catch it for him." Not far away, Mole noticed Mouse chasing after something that looked very much like a star.

"It's Mouse's star," he thought. "I'll help him catch it."

Up and up the hill ran Mole and
Mouse, until they reached the top.
But the leaf was already high in
the sky, glimmering in the autumn
sunshine. It swayed this way and
that, as if waving good-bye, and
then vanished altogether.

"The star has gone back to the sky," said Mouse.

"That's where it belongs," said Mole.

"Maybe it's for the best," sighed Mouse.

"I'm sure it is," agreed Mole.

There was a moment's silence.

"Anyway, we don't need a star.
We have each other," said Mouse.

"Of course we do," agreed Mole.

They gave each other a big hug, and then they lay back on top of the hill, feeling the wind. With their arms and legs stretched out, they looked just like two furry stars.